NORTH FAIRYLAND

BLUEBIRD HAVEN

COBHAM HILL

THE NARROWS

EAST BRIDGE

BROKENSTRAW CREEK

VILLAGE GARDEN

FAIRYGROUNDS

OLD RIVERTON INN

Map of Fairyland

FROG HOLLOW

Merry Christmas Ronan 2008
with lots of love
from
Frances May and Ian
xxx

Gather 'Round, 'tis Fairy Story Hour.

Written by
Mark Kimball Moulton

Art by
Karen Hillard good

©Copyright 2004

The Lang Companies, LLC

All Rights Reserved. Printed in the U.S.A.
514 Wells Street ~ Delafield, WI 53018
800.262.2611 ~ www.lang.com

10 9 8 7 6 5 4 3 2 1
ISBN: 0-7412-1940-9

KAREN,
THE
ILLUSTRATOR
(I'm
NOT
THAT
SKINNY.)

We
WANT
TO
Thank
All
the
Believers
OF
FAIRIES

MARK,
←THE
AUTHOR
(I'm not
THAT
CUTE.)

Fairy Facts

Fairies live in
oak trees (mostly).

THEY LOVE TO PLAY gAMES.

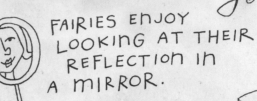

FAIRIES ENJOY
LOOKING AT THEIR
REFLECTION IN
A MIRROR.

THEIR FAVORITE
DESSERT
IS CAKE.

Fairies like to bathe
in cabbage leaves.

WHEN YOU HEAR THE WIND IN A WILLOW TREE,
IT IS SAID TO BE THE WHISPER OF A FAIRY
INTO THE EAR OF A POET.

SOME OF THE FLOWERS THAT FAIRIES LOVE:

BLUEBELLS... when fairies hear
bluebells ringing, that means
it's time to dance.

PANSY... used to make
love potions.

DAISY... great for tickling.

FOXGLOVES... especially good
for making hats and gloves.

PRIMROSE... if you place primroses
on your doorstep, fairies will visit
you at night and bless you while
you sleep.

They LOVE, LOVE, LOVE music!

ENTICE FAIRIES INTO YOUR
GARDEN BY BUILDING FAIRY HOUSES.
SIMPLY USE YOUR IMAGINATION
AND GIFTS FROM NATURE. FOR
EXAMPLE: MAKE A ROCK RING,
LEAVING A SMALL OPENING FOR FAIRIES TO ENTER, THEN LAY ON
A ROOF OF BARK. YOU COULD ALSO CREATE A STRUCTURE OF
BARK AND ADORN IT WITH LEAVES, ACORNS, BERRIES, ETC.
THE ONE THING THAT FAIRIES ARE VERY PARTICULAR ABOUT
IS THAT WE USE ONLY BUILDING MATERIALS FOUND IN NATURE!
THEN JUST WAIT AND BELIEVE!

A Fairy Poem
FROM IRELAND

'TIS THE MIDNIGHT HOUR!
THE MOON HANGS WHITE!
MORTAL BE WARE,
'TIS FAIRY NIGHT!

WITH MUSIC SWEET
AND LAUGHTER SHRILL,
'TIS PARTY TIME
ON FAIRY HILL!

written By
mark Kimball
moulton
illustrated By
Karen Hillard
good

Lang Books

Mr.
sparrow's
merry
Fairy
circus

Late one moonlit summer eve, I tossed and turned in bed,
  bothered by a problem that kept running through my head.

It really wasn't much at all, not worth a moment's thought,
  but lately things had bothered me more than I thought they ought.

"PEEP!"

Not long ago, when I was young, no problems bothered me,
but over time I found sleep harder than it used to be.

And just when I had started to begin to fall asleep,
I woke to what I thought to be a short, sharp whistled "PEEP!"

"PEEEEEP!"

"Rat-a-Tat-Tat-Tat!"

And then I heard a longer "PEEEEEP"
and one more after that-
followed by what sounded like a "Rat-a-Tat-Tat-Tat!"

Curious, I rose from bed and peered into the night-
only to be met by the most fascinating sight. . .

For there, among my garden flowers, lit softly by the moon,
I saw a four-piece fairy band prepared to play a tune!

Another fairy
stood upon a stool,
straight as an arrow.

He bowed
and introduced himself
to me as Mr. Sparrow!

He seemed to be a friendly,
most distinguished
English bloke-
apparently the leader
of these merry fairy folk.

He wore a red tuxedo coat
and tall, black stovepipe hat,
and all around his neck
there was a ruffled
white cravat.

The band members wore playful clothes that shimmered when they moved,
and pink petunia hats that, when they saw me, they removed.

One by one the fairies bowed and on their backs I saw,
wings like those on dragonflies. I stared, slack-jawed, in awe.

They had the cutest pointed ears and sparkling emerald eyes,
and smiles that looked as if they were in permanent surprise!

Their cheeks were plump as pillows and as pink as garden roses,
and every one of them had teensy-weensy turned up noses.

They stood about six inches tall, were round as chickadees,
and had the most adorable, distinctive knobby knees!

Each fairy held an instrument, no two of them the same-
a horn, a drum, a glockenspiel and one I couldn't name.

"Tap-tap! Peep! Peep! Tinkle! Toot! Toot!"

their music filled the air-
I found myself enamored by this Sousa-like affair!

*FAIRIES SHOWN ACTUAL SIZE.

They marched
   around the chamomile
and through the four-o'clocks,
   until they reached the center
      of three circles made of rocks.

A shadow crept across the moon, the band became real quiet-
   I held my breath, excited by the scene, I can't deny it.

Then all at once, like magic, those dark clouds were whisked away,
   and moonlight shone upon those rings, about as bright as day.

Mr. Sparrow's voice rang out, projected crystal clear.
   It sang throughout the garden
      loud enough for all to hear-

"Laadieeees and Gentlemen
and Children, if you please-focus on the center ring-
   I present the Great Trapeze!"

With that the drummer drummed his drum-

"Rat-a-tat-Tat-tat-tat-Tat!"
and from above there flew a little fairy acrobat!

Center Ring

He (or she, for honestly,
it was quite hard to tell),
came swinging from a swing
tied near the top of my bluebells!

The band struck up a swaying tune
that kept time with his act.
He swung around, then upside down,
hung by his feet, in fact!

She (or he) flew through the air to catch another swing,
then did a somersault to land inside that first rock ring.

A thousand little clapping hands and cheers and whistles, too,
erupted from my four-o'clocks, my lavender and rue.

I jumped, surprised and startled, unaware that they were there,
but all throughout my garden there were fairies everywhere!

YEAH!

They sat upon
the lemon thyme,
crossed-legged around the phlox,
they hung among the adder's-tongue
and sat on every rock.

Sometime between the marching band
and this, the Great Trapeze,
zillions of these little folk
had come in twos and threes.

Each one was dressed in playful clothes;
each one had emerald eyes.
Each one had little knobby knees;
each shimmered like sunrise.

Tiny candle lanterns hung from every flower stem,
dancing on each fairy's face, illuminating them.

The trapeze artist bowed to me,
then to her left and right,
then somersaulted out of sight
to everyone's delight!

Ring 1

YIPPEE!

HOORAY!

How dashing he (or she) had been,
performing with such ease.
Then Mr. Sparrow called to all the circus devotees-

"And now, my friends, the far left ring-an act that's death-defying...
The one and only Zora will perform her Dragon-Flying!!"

From shadows, there appeared a dragonfly of great proportions.
(Or was it just the shadows that had caused such great distortion?)

And on its back, there rode a fairy with the fairest hair,
who bravely rode that dragonfly straight up into the air!

Much like the bucking broncos of America's Wild West,
she fought that giant dragonfly and put it to the test!

One hand held straight up to the sky, the other holding tight,
she rode that dragonfly as he performed a reckless flight.

The fairies gasped and
"oohed" and "aahed"
as Zora tamed the brute.
He tried his best to throw her off
but she was resolute.

HA-HA-HA!

While at the same time,
in ring three,
two fairy clowns appeared,
mimicking the dragonfly
as he kicked, bucked and reared.

One rode upon the other's back.
They romped
and acted silly;
Chasing, teasing,
running round in circles

willy-nilly.

Ring 3

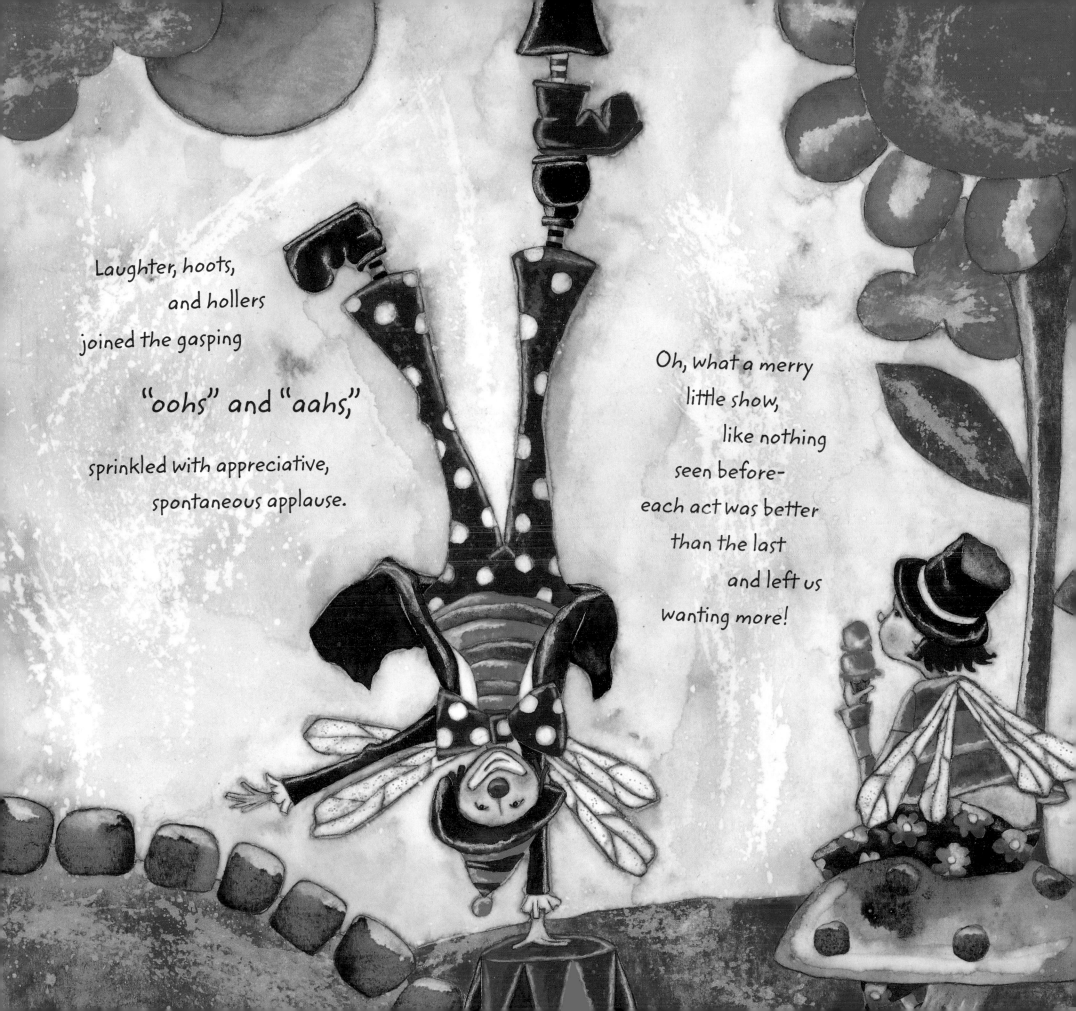

Laughter, hoots,
and hollers
joined the gasping

"oohs" and "aahs,"

sprinkled with appreciative,
spontaneous applause.

Oh, what a merry
little show,
like nothing
seen before-
each act was better
than the last
and left us
wanting more!

There were jugglers with acorns
and wild berries for their props,
and clowns who ran around the crowd
dressed up as Keystone Cops!

There were fairies high above
who balanced bravely on a thread,
and dancing fairies who wore plumes
of feathers on their heads!

Circus Tonight

But my favorite show of all,
the one I thought was awfully nice,
was the one that featured fairies
doing tricks with tame field mice.

They had them sit, they had them beg,
they had them jump through hoops,
and at the end the fairies
had them bow as one big group!   HOW CUTE!

And all the while the Ringmaster
led everyone in song,
accompanying the fairies' acts
throughout the whole nightlong.

I've no idea how long they stayed that magic summer eve,
but sometime late that night they all began to take their leave.

First Mr. Sparrow and his band addressed the fairy crowd.
They thanked us all for coming, and then one by one they bowed.

Then Mr. Sparrow looked at me and gave a subtle wink,
and made this observation which was meant for me, I think-

"Laaadieees and Gentlemen…"

"We hope you all enjoyed the show.
It's truly been our pleasure!
Performing for you here has been
an honor without measure!"

"We leave you now with memories
and this one final thought-
There are treasures in this world that
are so rare they can't be bought…"

"Dewdrops on a blade of grass and animals in clouds.
Dragonflies on lily pads and spring fields freshly plowed."

"And health and friends and family, don't take all this for granted,
along with the most precious gift-the gift to be enchanted..."

"We hope our little show tonight has helped you see this truth-
that you must always hold onto the magic of your youth!"

"For with this "magic view" in mind,
mere "life" becomes surreal-
dragonflies are bucking broncs
and lilies wear chenille!"

"And fairies really do exist
on moonlit summer eves-
for "life" appears exactly
as the way it is perceived!"

"We bid you a fond farewell...
Goodnight."

The band struck up another "March"
and then that small parade,
marched through my blue forget-me-nots
and down the path they'd made.

And one by one the audience of fairies vanished, too,
in tiny puffs of colored smoke in shades of pink and blue.

And all they left within their wake were tiny drops of dew,
that sparkled in the moonlight like real precious emeralds do.

I rubbed my eyes and blinked and when I slowly shook my head—
I found myself alone, awake in my own comfy bed!

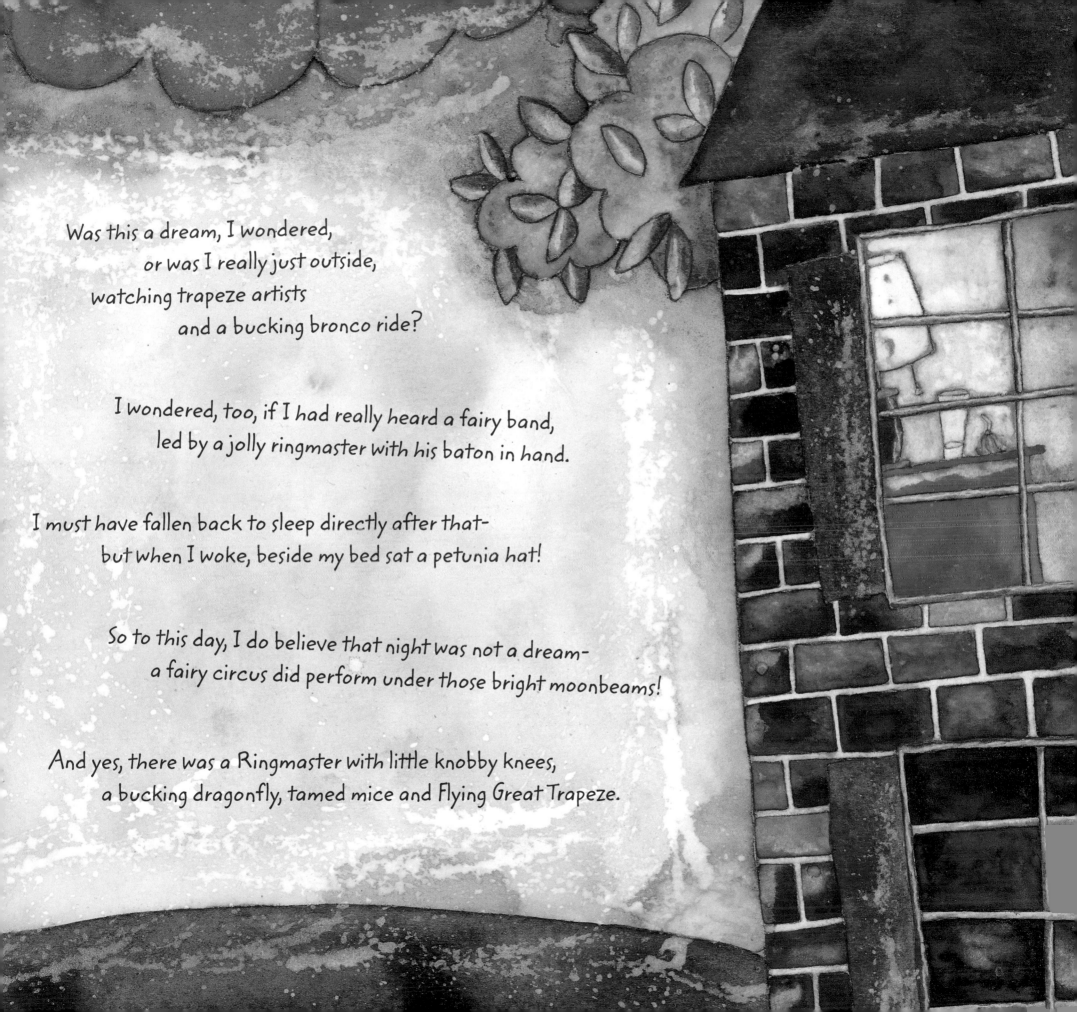

Was this a dream, I wondered,
        or was I really just outside,
watching trapeze artists
        and a bucking bronco ride?

I wondered, too, if I had really heard a fairy band,
        led by a jolly ringmaster with his baton in hand.

I must have fallen back to sleep directly after that—
        but when I woke, beside my bed sat a petunia hat!

So to this day, I do believe that night was not a dream—
        a fairy circus did perform under those bright moonbeams!

And yes, there was a Ringmaster with little knobby knees,
        a bucking dragonfly, tamed mice and Flying Great Trapeze.

And now I see those animals in clouds on summer days,
and spend whole afternoons just picking violet bouquets.

And jump rope when I want to, and play hopscotch in the road,
and listen to the blue jay's call and even talk to toads!

No longer do I toss and turn when I get into bed,
nor let some silly problem roll around inside my head.

For everything is magical, I've come to see the truth—

That life is truly Beautiful
Seen through the eyes
of youth.

The End

CRYSTAL LAKE

FAIRY QUEENIES CASTLE

PEEK N' PEEK MOUNTAINS

DEAD END

RIVER BEND

SMUGGLER'S NOTCH

EAST MIDDLE BRIDGE

WEST BRIDGE

N
W E
S

APPLE GROVE

ICE SKATING POND

TO TOWN WHERE THE PEOPLE LIVE (2.5 MILES FROM HERE)